San Francisco Public Library

P9-DYE-982

DEC 2009

DEMCO

Buenos días, buenas noches
Good Morning, Good Night

Escrito y ilustrado por Michael Grejniec
Written and illustrated by Michael Grejniec

Traducido por Alis Alejandro
Translated by Alis Alejandro

NORTHSOUTH
BOOKS

New York

Es de noche.
It is dark.

Es de día.
It is light.

Buenos días.
Good morning.

Estoy adentro.
I am inside.

Estoy afuera.
I am outside.

Estoy escondida.
I am hiding.

Estoy buscando.
I am seeking.

Tengo uno.

I have one.

Tengo muchos.
I have many.

Estoy abajo.
I am low.

Estoy arriba.
I am high.

¡Qué calma!
It is quiet.

¡Qué ruido!
It is noisy.

Estamos separados.
We are far.

Estamos juntos.
We are close.

Buenas noches.
Good night.

Copyright © 1993 by Michael Grejniec
First published in English under the title *Good Morning, Good Night*
Spanish translation copyright © 1997 by North-South Books Inc., New York

All rights reserved. No part of this book may be reproduced or utilized in any form or by any means,
electronic or mechanical, including photocopying, recording, or any information storage and retrieval system,
without permission in writing from the publisher.

First Spanish edition published in the United States and Canada in
1997 by Ediciones Norte-Sur, an imprint of NordSüd Verlag AG, Zürich Switzerland.
Distributed in the United States by North-South Books Inc., New York.

Library of Congress Cataloging-in-Publication Data is available.

ISBN-13: 978-0-7358-2109-5 / ISBN-10: 0-7358-2109-7 (library edition)
10 9 8 7 6 5 4 3 2 1

ISBN-13: 978-0-7358-2110-1 / ISBN-10: 0-7358-2110-0 (paperback edition)
10 9 8 7 6 5 4 3 2 1

Printed in Belgium